RICHARD SCARRY'S
Great Big Schoolhouse
Readers

Cake Soup

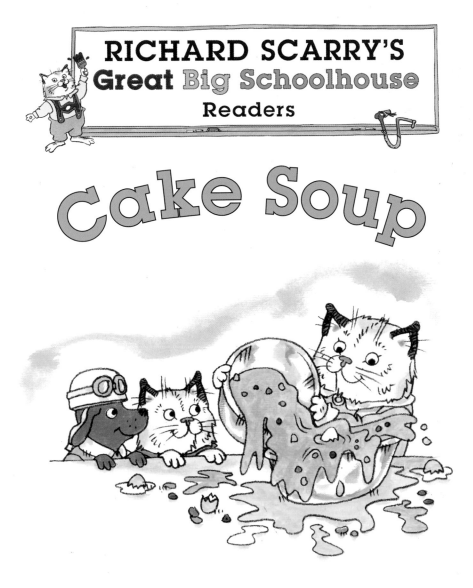

Illustrated by Huck Scarry
Written by Erica Farber

STERLING

New York / London
www.sterlingpublishing.com/kids

It is Lowly's birthday.

Time to make the cake.

In goes the mix.
In goes the milk.
Oh, no!

3

Next go the eggs.

One egg. Two eggs.

Three eggs. Lots of eggs!

This cake is not good.

It needs ice cream.

It needs candy.

It needs juice.

Time to bake the cake.

Bake, cake, bake!

Here come the balloons.

Whoosh! Oh, no!

Molly and Ella get ready.

Bake, cake, bake!

Oh, no!

Skip's present is walking away.

Uh, oh!

There goes Frances's present.

BOOM! Look out!

Bake, cake, bake!

Ding-dong! It is Lowly.

Happy birthday, Lowly!

Time to take out the cake.

Here comes the cake.

That cake is not cake!

It is soup.

Cake soup for everyone.
Yum! Yum!

It is the best birthday
cake ever!

STERLING and the distinctive Sterling logo are registered trademarks of Sterling Publishing Co., Inc.

Library of Congress Cataloging-in-Publication Data Available

Lot #: 10 9 8 7 6 5
02/15
Published by Sterling Publishing Co., Inc.
387 Park Avenue South, New York, NY 10016

In association with JB Publishing, Inc.
41 River Terrace, New York, New York

Text © 2011 JB Publishing, Inc.
Illustrations © 2011 Richard Scarry Corporation
All characters are the property of the Richard Scarry Corporation.

Distributed in Canada by Sterling Publishing
c/o Canadian Manda Group, 165 Dufferin Street
Toronto, Ontario, Canada M6K 3H6
Distributed in the United Kingdom by GMC Distribution Services
Castle Place, 166 High Street, Lewes, East Sussex, England BN7 1XU
Distributed in Australia by Capricorn Link (Australia) Pty. Ltd.
P.O. Box 704, Windsor, NSW 2756, Australia

produced by ●JR Sansevere

Printed in China
All rights reserved

Sterling ISBN: 978-1-4027-8446-0 (hardcover)
            978-1-4027-7317-4 (paperback)

For information about custom editions, special sales, premium and corporate purchases, please contact Sterling Special Sales Department at 800-805-5489 or specialsales@sterlingpublishing.com.

RICHARD SCARRY'S
Great Big Schoolhouse
Readers

One of the best-selling children's author/illustrators of all time, Richard Scarry has taught generations of children about the world around them—from the alphabet to counting, identifying colors, and even exploring a day at school.

Though Scarry's books are educational, they are beloved for their charming characters, wacky sense of humor, and frenetic energy. Scarry considered himself an entertainer first, and an educator second. He once said, "Everything has an educational value if you look for it. But it's the FUN I want to get across."

A prolific artist, Richard Scarry created more than 300 books, and they have sold over 200 million copies worldwide and have been translated into 30 languages. Richard Scarry died in 1994, but his incredible legacy continues with new books illustrated by his son, Huck Scarry.

Bake, cake, bake!

It is Lowly's birthday. Time to make the cake.

Oh, no! That is not cake.

It is soup!

Find out Huckle and Bridget's secret recipe

for the best birthday cake ever!

LEVEL 1 Introduce Your Child to Reading

LEVEL 2 Your Child Starts to Read

LEVEL 3 Your Child Reads with Help

STERLING

New York / London
www.sterlingpublishing.com/kids

$3.95 / Can. $

ISBN 978-1-4027-73

9 781402 773174

W8-BUP-032